THE
MYSTERY
OF THE
STOLEN JEWELS

THE
MYSTERY
OF THE
STOLEN JEWELS

AND OTHER ROYAL ADVENTURES
Compiled by the Editors
of
Highlights for Children

CONTENTS

The Mystery of the Stolen Jewels
by Linda J. Anthony...7

A Fairly Fairy Tale by Julianne French.............13

The Doll Maker by Beth M. Applegate 19

Smart Sir Day and the Slipping Stable
by Nancy Garber 27

Garden for a King by Marilyn Kratz.................31

The King Who Commanded the Tide
by Margaret Maddox Wallworth 35

Soda-Cracker Kingdom by Margaret Welsh ...39

The Princess and the Tiger
by Sara Thompson...45

300 Oranges by Alfred Taylor............................51

Prince Fennepin's Crown
by June Swanson...59

The Princess and the Star by Toby Speed....63

King Frederick the Undignified
by Diana Logue 67

From Up Above by Maia Rodman.......................73

A Song for the King by Marilyn Kratz 79

The Island That Had No Birds
by Sister Mary Terese Donze, A.S.C. 85

A Shovel, an Ax, and a Ladder
by Walter K. Putney 91

THE
MYSTERY
OF THE
STOLEN JEWELS

By Linda J. Anthony

"Hear ye! Hear ye!" the Royal Messenger proclaimed. "The Royal Jewels have disappeared—stolen by person or persons unknown!" A reward notice, signed by the King and Queen, soon appeared on doorways: Find the Jewels and Anything—Within Reason—Is Yours.

Throughout the kingdom, each person vowed to solve the theft and collect the reward.

Even Rufus, the Twenty-third Under-Assistant Pigkeeper at the Royal Piggery, declared that he would find the jewels.

"A bumbling buffoon like you?" laughed the Fourteenth Under-Assistant Pigkeeper. "Ridiculous!"

"You? Dim-witted Rufus?" snickered the Eighth Under-Assistant Pigkeeper. "Why, you can't even find matching socks in the morning." The other pigkeepers rolled on the ground, laughing and slapping their knees.

"We'll see," Rufus said. "I am as cunning as the next man."

"Hush!" someone said. "The Head Pigkeeper returns." Quickly, the pigkeepers busied themselves with their piggery chores.

"Rufus!" roared the Head Pigkeeper.

"Yes, Master."

"You'll be on guard duty through the night."

"B-b-but, Sir," protested Rufus. "I worked all day!"

The Head Pigkeeper frowned a terrible frown. "If you wish to retain your position, you will do as you are told."

"When will I look for the Royal Jewels?" Rufus thought. But he dared not say a word.

That night, while the Royal Pigs snored, Rufus leaned against the fence and stifled a yawn. "How many more hours?" he wondered. "Will morning never come?"

Gently, his eyes began to close. Slowly he slipped to the ground. Soon his snores mingled with the grunts of sleeping pigs. *Find the Jewels,* he dreamed, *and anything—within reason—is yours. The Jewels, the Jewels . . .*

"Where are the Jewels?" whispered a gruff voice nearby. Rufus did not move, but his eyes flew wide open.

"Here," a sharp voice answered. "Act quickly now, before we're discovered."

The sounds Rufus heard were not the nighttime noises made by pigs in the Royal Piggery. He heard a sharp clink of metal against stone, a dull thud of dirt, and a muffled grunt. Cautiously, Rufus peeked round the corner of the fence.

In the moonlight he saw a man crouched over a hole. Next to the man stood a woman wrapped in a dark cloak. A glint of gold flashed from a box she held in her arms.

"Hurry!" whispered the woman. She poked at the man with her silk-slippered foot.

"Ooomph," the man said. "I'm digging as fast as I can."

The woman looked over her shoulder. "What's that noise?"

"Nothing, nothing. Only the pigs, rooting in their sleep."

Rufus sank down behind the fence and closed his eyes. The Royal Jewel Thieves!

Rufus heard a few more thumps and a shoosh of dirt. Then the man said, "Finished." His breathing became easier. "Meet me here when the uproar about the theft dies down," he told the woman. "Then the two of us will disappear. No one will be the wiser."

"We will be rich," the woman whispered. "Rich!" With a swish of her silk skirts, she was gone.

Rufus held his breath.

But wait! Footsteps approached the very spot where Rufus lay. He snapped his eyes shut and uttered a deep snore.

The man stopped short and poked at Rufus with his boot. Rufus grunted and turned over, letting out another snore.

"Dim-witted Rufus," the man said. "Sleeping on the job, eh? Just as I expected." With a nasty chuckle, the man disappeared.

Rufus sat up. He knew that voice! It belonged to the Head Pigkeeper!

The next morning, Rufus strode boldly into the Royal Antechamber. He handed the Royal Jewel Box, splotched with dirt and smelling faintly of pig, to the Lord Chamberlain.

"Return on the morrow to collect your reward," Rufus was told. "You may have anything you want—within reason, of course."

Word travels fast in a small kingdom. The next morning a crowd gathered at the castle gate and watched enviously as Rufus strutted into the Royal Chamber.

"You may have anything you like," the Queen told Rufus.

"Within reason," added the King.

Without a pause or a stammer, Rufus stated his request.

The Queen looked at the King.

The King looked at the Queen.

"Why not?" said the King.

"It's clearly within reason," the Queen observed. "Why not, indeed!" She beamed at Rufus. "Your wish is granted."

Rufus could not believe his good fortune. He emerged from the Royal Chamber with a dazed smile upon his face.

"What is your reward?" someone asked him. "Gold coins? A diamond ring? A coach-and-four, perhaps?" The people fell silent, waiting for Rufus to speak.

Rufus told them what he had wished for, and his voice rang with pride. But the people looked at each other in amazement as his words sank in.

"Fool," said a man. "You could have asked for anything you wanted—within reason, of course."

"Trust dim-witted Rufus to waste a good oppor-
tunity," called another, and the people began to
laugh.

For once, the Royal Pigkeepers did not join in the
laughter. Instead, they kept a stunned and respectful
silence.

Rufus ignored the crowd. "Come along," he said
to the pigkeepers. "There's work to be done."

The pigkeepers meekly followed Rufus, who
led them back to the Royal Piggery. No one dared
argue with the kingdom's new Head Pigkeeper.

A Fairly Fairy Tale

By Julianne French

Melville and his father, the king, had just started a game of chess when a page entered the room.

"There's a woodchopper here at Trembly with a strange tale," said the page.

The woodchopper stepped forward and, holding his cap in his hands, knelt before the king.

"I was going out to chop wood on the other side of the mountain when I came upon a castle," the woodchopper explained. "Guarded by a fierce dragon, it was. Inside the gate I spied a beautiful girl. I'm sure she's a princess, and the dragon is holding her captive."

Springing to his feet, Melville shouted, "I'll rescue her!"

The king shook his head. "You're the youngest," he said. "I'll send one of your older brothers."

"Why waste all that time, Dad?" said Melville. "The youngest son always wins the princess."

"That is true," agreed the woodchopper.

"Hmm," the king said, stroking his beard as he thought.

Then he put his arm around Melville's shoulder.

"All right, go ahead. But be careful; it's your first dragon."

Melville hurriedly packed a bag of provisions and went out to where his horse, Compass, was stabled. Melville mounted Compass, and they headed for the forest.

Soon Melville saw an old woman sitting outside a hut, spinning. From what he had heard of these adventures, the old woman was probably a witch. Opening his bag, Melville searched until he found a raspberry tart.

"Here, old woman, you look hungry," said Melville, handing her the tart.

"Why, thank you, sonny," the woman said. "That'll taste good with my supper."

"I'm looking for a castle guarded by a dragon," said Melville.

"You must mean Burnt Moats," the woman said, pointing north. "It's over there."

Compass started off at a gallop, and the pair cut through the forest. Before long, Melville saw a castle with a dragon standing at the gate. Melville sneaked up behind the dragon. Just as he was about to grab the scaly creature by the tail, someone shouted, "Leave Goliath alone!"

Melville jumped, and his mouth dropped open. "You must be the princess," he said.

"I'm not a princess," the girl answered. "Since my parents died, I'm the queen."

"Well, Queen—" Melville began.

"Call me Wisteria," she said.

"Well, Wisteria," Melville began again, "I came to rescue you from the dragon and win you for my bride."

"Rescue me from Goliath!" Wisteria started to laugh. "He's my friend."

"There must be some way I can serve you," said Melville. "There must be something you want."

Wisteria looked wistful.

"Jewels?" suggested Melville.

"I never wear them," Wisteria said. "I'd just lose them riding in the forest."

Then she turned to the dragon and gave him a friendly pat. "After the way you treated Goliath, perhaps you could do a favor for him. He likes to putter around in the garden. Why don't you get him some fish shells?"

Melville swept off his hat and bowed politely to Queen Wisteria. Then he mounted Compass and headed back at a gallop toward the old woman's hut. When he got there, she was still sitting outside, spinning.

"The queen of Burnt Moats wants some fish shells," said Melville.

"Fish shells?" the woman said. "Fish have scales. It sounds like some kind of riddle to me."

"That's why I thought you could help," said Melville. "Being a witch—"

"A what!" said the woman. "It's lucky for you my sons are at sea."

"I didn't mean to insult you," said Melville.

The woman snorted. "I'm no witch, but if you want my advice, you'll go back and ask the queen what she means."

"I've never heard of anyone on a quest doing a thing like that," Melville said.

"Suit yourself, sonny," she said. "But I don't know how you can find what you're looking for if you don't know what it is."

Without waiting for Melville to make up his mind, Compass turned around and galloped back to Burnt Moats.

"Tell me what the queen says," the woman called after them. "I'm curious myself."

Before he reached the castle, Melville saw Wisteria and Goliath in a clearing. Wisteria was practicing archery.

"I forgot to ask you what fish shells are," said Melville. "Are they some kind of flower?"

"No," said Wisteria, laughing. "They look a bit like snail shells, except they come from the sea. Goliath wants to line the garden path with them."

Once more Compass turned Melville toward the old woman's hut. When they arrived, Melville told her what Wisteria had said.

"Oh, she wants some seashells," the woman said. "She must have seen the ones lining my path. The boys brought them to me. I think they're so pretty that I collect them. Come on in."

Melville followed her inside the hut. The woman opened a trunk filled with seashells and put some in a sack. Then she gave the sack to Melville.

As Melville loaded the sack on Compass, he said, "You've certainly made my quest easy for me."

"Well, somebody had to. You've tried to make it hard enough for yourself," she said.

Compass whinnied and started for Burnt Moats. Wisteria and Goliath were saddling a horse when Melville found them.

"We were just going on a picnic," said Wisteria.

"I hoped you could come home with me," said Melville. "I brought you the fish shells, thinking I could win you for my bride."

"You got the fish shells for Goliath," Wisteria said. "And I'm not sure Goliath will marry you."

Goliath thought that was so funny he began to chuckle, and green smoke puffed from his nose.

Hanging his head, Melville said, "You're right. But now I'll have to go back home and marry some dull, proper princess that Dad chooses for me. And I love you."

"Why didn't you say so in the first place?" asked Wisteria. "It would have saved a lot of time."

The Doll Maker

By Beth M. Applegate

The ax bit sharply into the cedar log, and the wood parted with a crackling sound in the cold December air. A large wood chip flew through the air and landed at young Tobias Treslin's feet. Tobias picked it up and examined it. A knot in the wood bulged out, making it look like a child's face, and darker portions resembled warm brown eyes that appeared to be gazing at him. His thin face broke into a smile.

"I'll use this for a doll's head," Tobias thought.

"I'll carve the body and fix it for Suzette. She's never had a doll." He dropped the piece of wood into his pocket and picked up his ax.

The long day was finally ending. Tobias had worked since dawn on the marquis's land, chopping wood for the huge castle fireplaces. Tomorrow and the day after that he would be hauling the wood to the castle.

"If there were only more time for woodcarving and for fixing our own house," Tobias murmured to himself as he started for home across the crusted snow. "But a serf must give his three days each week to his lord. 'Tis not fair. My mother has only rags to wear and Suzette has not a single toy, while those at the castle have more than they need."

He turned into the yard at his mother's cottage, still grumbling to himself. "If I could find work in one of the guilds in Lyon I could help us all. But should a runaway serf be caught, he would be thrown into the dungeon."

"Toby, Toby," little Suzette called, running to greet him.

"Tobias." His mother smiled. "You must be half frozen. Come in. Here, give me your coat and I'll hang it up for you. Ah, what is this in your pocket?" She pulled out the chip of wood and turned to the firelight. "What a curiously shaped piece," she exclaimed, holding it so that the warm fire-light danced on the wood. "It looks for all the world like a face."

"I thought so myself when I picked it up. I've a plan, Mother. A secret."

"Tell me! Tell me!" Suzette begged.

"If I did, it wouldn't be a secret," Tobias smiled. "Let's eat, Mother. I'm starved."

It was not until Suzette was fast asleep that Tobias told his mother his plan. "I'll make legs and arms out of straight, strong wood. You can sew a dress for it. She will be a fine doll."

"You are very clever with your knife, Tobias. You'll do it well."

"I'll joint the legs and arms so they'll move, Mother."

"I'll find scraps of material for clothing," Mrs. Treslin smiled. "But go to bed now. It is getting very late."

The following day Tobias and two others from the village went to deliver the wood to the castle. With the Christmas holidays approaching, every fireplace would be lighted for the many guests who would be staying with the lord.

During the noon hour, Tobias and his companions sat against a sunny wall in the outer court. Tobias brought a long piece of wood from his pocket. Carefully he shaped the doll's legs and feet with his knife. He then rounded the edges of a square piece of wood for the body and attached the arms and legs to it. Finally, he gently added the beautiful wooden head.

That evening he showed it to his mother. "Why, Tobias," she exclaimed. "It looks exactly as a small child should. Feet and hands, too! It's beautiful."

"I'll have it ready for Christmas," Tobias said as his mother took the measurements for tiny garments.

He took the doll with him the following day, and again used his noon lunch hour to carve upon it. This time he shaped the hair above the eyes. He was so interested in his work that he did not hear approaching footsteps.

"Well, serf," a cold voice said. "Have you not the good manners to bow to your betters?"

Tobias sprang to his feet, dropping the wooden doll onto the stones of the courtyard with a clatter. Before him stood a tall, dark boy of about fourteen. He was Leon, the marquis's son. Beside him stood his small sister, Ellen.

"I . . . I . . . a thousand pardons, sire." Tobias's face turned scarlet as he quickly bowed to the older boy.

"And what have we here?" Leon asked, picking up the doll.

"It's a doll!" Ellen cried. "A doll that moves. Let me have it. See, it dances! It dances!"

Tobias reached for the doll. "It's for my sister."

But Leon handed the doll to the girl. "Here, Ellen. You may have it."

Tobias stepped forward to retrieve the doll and received a stinging slap on the face.

"Would you take a doll from a small child?" Leon asked.

"But, sire, the doll is mine. It's my sister's Christmas present. She has never had a doll."

"The Lady Ellen wishes this doll, and she shall have it."

"No!" Again Tobias reached for the doll. But the small girl held the doll close.

"Be off with you, pig," Leon snapped.

"I am not a pig, and you have stolen my doll," Tobias shouted. His fist shot out, striking the tall boy on the chin and knocking him to the pavement.

"Tobias!" called one of the woodsmen, who had been watching the scene. "Stop! Get out of here before you are in more trouble. The marquis will have you thrown into the dungeon. Run, Tobias!"

Suddenly Tobias realized what he had done. He had struck his master's son! Fear possessed him. He ran through the courtyard gate and down the road to the village.

Hot with anger, he burst into his home. "They took the doll! They took the doll!" he shouted. "Leon took the doll from me and gave it to Lady Ellen. And I struck him!"

"Tobias!" His mother's mouth fell open in horror. "What are you saying? How could you strike the marquis's son? We will all be punished."

"I'll run away," said Tobias. "They cannot punish you and Suzette for what I did. I will run away tonight, as soon as it is dark. I'll try to find work with one of the guild masters. I must hide now. But where? Where?"

"Under the thatch in the attic," said his mother. "Oh, Toby boy, why did you do it?"

All that afternoon Tobias lay in the darkness of the attic, waiting for the dusk to settle in. Early in the evening he crept down and dressed himself warmly for the long journey that was ahead of him.

"It will be a sad Christmas for us all," his mother sighed. Suzette clung to him, begging him not to go.

He was almost ready to set out when he heard the sound of horses' hooves thundering down the lane. The horses stopped outside the cottage.

"Hide, Toby!" whispered his mother.

"Open the door! Open up!" a voice barked.

Mrs. Treslin opened the door and bowed low to the marquis and his companion.

"Is your son here?" the marquis asked.

"He . . . he went to work this morning with the foresters," Mrs. Treslin said nervously.

"But he returned this evening. He must be here."

"You have come to punish him," Mrs. Treslin protested. "He was not the guilty one. He meant no harm. It was his doll. Please, please! He is only a lad, and my only support!"

"But it is about the doll that we came to see him," said the marquis's companion. "I am Jacques Michel of Lyon, a carver of statues. Your son's doll shows much talent. I should like to take him with me to Lyon as my apprentice. I will see that he is well fed and clothed. The marquis will look after you and your little one."

"He will not be punished, sire?"

The marquis shook his head. "Sometimes my son is hot-headed and thoughtless."

Tobias burst out of the corner. "Mother, Mother," he said. "I would be so happy to learn to carve. I might make decorations for the church! It is what I have always wanted. To think that this could happen to me—a serf."

"And here is the doll," the marquis said gravely. "It was rightly yours, Tobias. Leon had no right to give it to small Ellen. But if you will make her one, I will pay you well."

"I will, sire, I will," Tobias promised, his eyes shining with happiness.

"And a happy Christmas to you all," the marquis said as he and his companion turned and started back to their horses.

SMART SIR DAY AND THE SLIPPING STABLE

By Nancy Garber

Once upon a time there lived a knight whose name was Day. Sir Day didn't bother with the things most of the other knights cared about. When he should have been practicing swordplay, dragon fighting, or jousting with the other knights, he was always doing something else. And the king and the other knights hardly spoke to him because of that.

Just yesterday Sir Day saved a donkey from a bear trap (and forgot to go out for sword drill).

Two days before that he rescued a well-digger who had fallen into a hole (and missed his Dragon Defense class).

And last week he watered a fern that was wilting (and splashed water on his armor so that it began to squeak when he walked).

Sir Day was telling himself he should be more careful when the king called the knights together.

"I am very upset," the king said, "to find that our stable is slipping."

"Sleeping?" asked Sir Day.

"No—slipping," said the king. "Slipping right down into the moat. The mud oozes out from under the stable, and the building slides down the hill, closer and closer to the moat."

"Goodness," said the queen, "I noticed something was different, but I thought it was only because I had eaten radishes."

"Please, Alyesa," said the king, "be quiet. You don't know anything about this."

The queen sighed.

Sir Day felt sorry for Aleysa. The king always talked to her like that—as if she didn't have a brain. And come to think of it, that was sort of the same way he talked to Sir Day.

Sir Day followed the queen down the hill. "May I help, Your Majesty?" he asked.

"No, Sir Day, unless you can help me think of a way to keep the stable from sleeping. I mean, from slipping."

"Well," he said, "we'll think of something."

The next day the biggest and handsomest knight in the kingdom tried *his* idea. He tied long ropes to the stable and wrapped them around some trees on the other side of the hill. But the ropes broke, and the stable slipped even farther.

Then a famous knight from the next kingdom rolled some boulders onto the hill and placed them under the stable. But the stable slid right up over them and slipped down another foot.

The king was annoyed. He went into the castle and slammed the door. The stable shook and slipped some more.

"All right," the queen said. "Now we shall put our plan into action."

Sir Day and the queen went down into the valley and through the forest. They took with them the donkey, a cart, and the well-digger man. When they came back around the mountain they had trees, bushes, and plants in the cart. They drove up near the side of the stable and dug holes and started to plant. They planted trees, evergreens, bushes, and all kinds of crawly green plants that spread on the ground. And they planted the fern Sir Day had rescued earlier. They put a few rocks here and there to help hold the soil.

Finally they attached a diving board to the edge of the moat because the king loved to swim.

When they had finished, the queen went in to get the king.

"Goodness, my dear," he said, "your hands are dirty and your face is covered with leaves. Whatever have you been doing?"

"I've been having the most fun, Harold," she said. "Come and see."

The king could hardly believe his eyes. The trees stood straight and tall, the bushes fanned out over the ground, the plants spread and flowed. The fern blew gently in the breeze, and the stable stood still.

"This is wonderful," he said. "How did you do it?"

"Sir Day and the well-digger man and the donkey and I—we did it together," the queen said. "We thought of it and we dug up all those plants and we planted them over there and—"

"And we put up the diving board," said Sir Day, holding very still so his armor wouldn't squeak.

The king was so happy he gave a great party in celebration of the stabilizing of the stable.

During the party the queen oiled Sir Day's armor, the king went swimming in the moat, and Sir Day rescued a squirrel from a wire cage.

GARDEN FOR A KING

By Marilyn Kratz

Everyone in Millville agreed that Mrs. Poppen had the most beautiful flower garden in town.

So when the king sent word he would visit Millville and would have tea in the town's most beautiful garden (because he loved flowers), everyone knew Mrs. Poppen would have the honor.

"And you deserve it," declared Mr. Florry. "There's never a weed in your marigold patch."

"Or a faded blossom on your morning-glory vine," said the town clerk, Myra Dunlop.

"Or an unsightly blight on your petunias," added Grandma Johnson.

"We are so proud to have your beautiful garden in our town," said Mayor Wumply.

"Thank you, dear friends," said Mrs. Poppen, who was very pleased. "I will be honored to serve tea to the king in my garden."

"Perhaps we should all plant some flowers in honor of the king's visit," said Mayor Wumply.

"But I don't know what kind of flowers would look nice around my brown house," said Mr. Florry.

"Most flowers make me sneeze," said Myra Dunlop. Just thinking of them made her "Ah-choo!"

"I can't tell the flowers from the weeds when they sprout," said Grandma Johnson. "I always pull the wrong ones."

"I will help you," said Mrs. Poppen, even though she had work to do in her own garden.

First, she helped Mr. Florry plant bright yellow and orange marigolds around his brown house.

"They make your house look so cheerful," she said.

The next day, Mrs. Poppen had just started weeding her garden when Myra Dunlop asked for some help. So Mrs. Poppen took a dozen morning-glory vines to Myra's house.

"Morning glories hardly ever make anyone sneeze," she assured Myra. But just to be safe, Myra tied a red handkerchief over her nose as she helped Ms. Poppen plant the vines along the fence.

The next day, Mrs. Poppen had just started to water her flowers when she remembered Grandma Johnson. So she took some petunia plants to Grandma Johnson's house.

"These petunias are covered with bright pink blossoms," said Mrs. Poppen. "You will have no trouble telling them from the weeds."

"Oh, I do hope none of my weeds have pink blossoms," worried Grandma Johnson.

As the days went by Mrs. Poppen helped many others plant flowers. In fact, she was so busy helping the others that she didn't have time for her own garden.

Then one day Mayor Wumply said, "Tomorrow the king will come! I'm sure he'll be delighted to see all the lovely flower gardens in Millville. I wonder where he'll choose to have tea."

Everyone else wondered, too. They all rushed home to make sure their gardens were as neat and pretty as possible.

But Mrs. Poppen did not rush home. She walked—very slowly—because she was very tired after all the weeding, watering, and hoeing she had done in other people's gardens.

When Mrs. Poppen reached her house, she looked sadly at her own weedy, neglected garden. Then she sighed and went in to get ready for bed. How honored she would have been to serve tea to the king in her very own garden. But she knew he would not choose her ugly, overgrown garden.

The sun was shining brightly the next morning when Mrs. Poppen was awakened by a loud pounding on her door.

"Wake up, Mrs. Poppen!" called Mayor Wumply. "The king wants to have tea in your garden!"

"What? That can't be!" Mrs. Poppen dressed hurriedly and rushed into her garden. She couldn't believe her eyes!

Her garden was full of flowers. There were bowls of flowers along the fence, baskets of flowers along the path, and vases of flowers around each tree. Even the wheelbarrow and watering can were full of flowers. And there wasn't a weed in sight!

All the people Mrs. Poppen had helped were there. They smiled as Mayor Wumply presented her to the king, saying, "This is Mrs. Poppen, Your Highness. Because she loves flowers as much as you do, there are gardens all over Millville now. And because we love her, we have brought our prettiest flowers to her garden today."

Mrs. Poppen looked around at her garden filled with flowers and friends. She was sure it had never looked more beautiful.

The King Who Commanded The Tide

By Margaret Maddox Wallworth

In the early days of his reign King Canute fought many battles, both in his kingdom of Calount and in the land of Mathir, in order to secure the crowns he claimed from both peoples. Whenever King Canute could avoid a battle, he did; but when he fought, he was usually victorious. The knights and advisors who surrounded him, and to whom he looked for good advice, began to praise King Canute for his wisdom and power. They encouraged him to seek out new conquests.

"You are the mightiest king," they bragged to him. "You have but to utter a command and the world must obey!"

King Canute looked at his advisors thoughtfully when they said such things. He knew that false pride was a very dangerous fault in a king and his counselors. He decided that he would teach them a lesson in humility.

"Come," he said one day in the midst of a council. "I wish to go to the seashore."

The advisors looked at one another in some confusion at King Canute's sudden whim, but they dared not question him. Quickly they summoned the servants and told them to bring food and drink and a comfortable chair for the king.

The party reached the seashore at that time of day when the tide was due to come in.

"Set my chair there," Canute ordered the servants. "I wish to gaze at the sunset over the water." He had his servants place the gorgeous gilded chair with its thick red cushion right in the path of the incoming tide.

The advisors looked at one another nervously and murmured, but only one had the courage to approach King Canute. "Pardon, Your Majesty," he whispered in the king's ear, "the tide is coming in, and you will soon be forced to move."

Canute looked at the man in feigned astonishment and fury.

"*Forced* to move!" he exclaimed. "Am I not the king? I have but to command the tide to stay while I choose to sit here. Let it dare to wet the royal foot! Am I not the king?"

The embarrassed nobleman retreated. King Canute settled himself comfortably in his chair.

Meanwhile, the tide moved closer to the spot where the king's chair stood. It was a yard from the royal slippers, then two feet, then only a foot away. King Canute spoke in a thundering voice. "Tide, I command thee to stop! I, the mightiest king in the land, command thee to stop right there!"

But the tide did not stop. Inch by inch it moved toward the king. The rich purple of his slippers darkened as the water lapped against them. The water was around the king's ankles now, and steadily rising. In terrible consternation, all of the king's advisors waded out to stand around him and steady the chair. Canute looked from his immersed feet to his advisors. A frown darkened his face. He spoke. "You see that I have commanded the tide, but it does not obey me."

The men could not meet the king's eyes.

"It would seem that even a king's commands are limited," said Canute. "I need men around me who

37

will remind me that I am a man—not flatterers who will deceive me into believing that I am a god."

In great shame, the advisers knelt in the water, drenching their fine clothes. "Forgiveness, Sire, forgiveness," they begged.

Canute rose from the chair, and the red cushion floated away.

"You are forgiven," he said. "Now let's get back to dry land before we all drown!"

From that day onward, Canute's advisors stopped their empty flattery and used their common sense in advising the king. And the king ruled wisely and well for many years.

Soda-Cracker Kingdom

By Margaret Welsh

Once upon a time a very foolish king ate too many soda crackers. His people ate them because their king ate them. The king ate them because his people ate them. And so on. They all ate so many that everyone turned into soda-cracker people. They used the rest of the crackers to build a castle for the royal family. That is how the soda-cracker kingdom came to be.

The castle was built upon the shore of Longest-Lake-in-the-World, across from Green Forest. For many years the soda-cracker king and his beautiful cracker daughter lived there in comfort. Often the king would go to the edge of Longest-Lake-in-the-World and listen to the songs of birds that lived in Green Forest.

One bird sang more beautifully than the others. The king could see it in the branches of the tallest tree. It was a wonderful sight to see. The bird seemed golden when the sun shone, and moonlight turned it to silver.

For many years the soda-cracker king had wished to own such a fine bird. How happy he would be if only the golden-silver bird would sing for him in the garden of the castle. Once the king had tried to wade across the lake to reach the forest and the bird. Alas! The minute he put one foot into the water, his toes washed away! It had taken the royal baker hours to bake five new toes suitable for a king.

After that, the king stayed in the garden of the castle. As he listened to the song of the golden-silver bird, he grew more and more unhappy.

At last the soda-cracker king sent for his many rich lords. The many rich lords sent for the busy men of business. The busy men of business sent for the handsome young page. Then all of them came to the great hall of the soda-cracker castle to listen to the words of the king.

The king wore his finest robe of strawberry frosting, with a red cherry crown to match. Climbing up on top of a marshmallow so he could be seen and heard by all, he spoke to the soda-cracker people:

Beyond the lake, high in a tree,
A beautiful bird sings a royal song.
To him who brings that bird to me,
Princess and kingdom do belong!

"The kingdom?" cried the many rich lords.

"The kingdom?" cried the busy men of business.

"The princess?" cried the handsome young page. "The beautiful princess whom I love so dearly?"

In the days that followed, the many rich lords went to the north, trying to find their way around Longest-Lake-in-the-World. All of the busy men of business went south, hoping to find their way in that direction. One by one they all came back, each to report sadly that the lake was indeed the longest in the world, for as far as any of them could see, it had no end at all.

All the while the lords and men of business were wasting their time running back and forth without thinking, the handsome young page was quietly planning what to do. He was willing to give his life, if need be, to be worthy of the beautiful royal princess. He went bravely to the edge of the lake and lay flat on the water, hoping to

41

float to the other shore before he washed away. Instead of washing away, to his great surprise, the soda-cracker page began to swell!

He grew
and grew
and GREW!

Soon his toes touched the edge of Green Forest, while his head rested on the shore of soda-cracker land. Slowly the young page stood up. To his amazement, he was more than twenty times his former size! He was much softer, too, for he had soaked up a great deal of water.

Carefully lifting one foot, the page took a step. It was such a big step (for now he was so much taller) that he found himself in the very center of Green Forest, quite close to the tallest tree. Wobbling back and forth on tiptoe, he was just able to reach the golden-silver bird. Taking the bird, the handsome page took three very wobbly steps and found himself back in the soda-cracker kingdom.

Lying on the hill in the warm sun, the handsome young page was very sad. He had the wonderful bird, but he was afraid to ask for the reward. Here he was, all swollen up, far too large even to go through the door of the castle. How could he claim the kingdom? How could he ask for the love of the princess?

As the sun shone upon the young page, it slowly began to warm him. The warmer he got, the stronger he felt. Could it be true that he was drying and shrinking? As he became warmer and drier, he grew

SMALLER

and SMALLER

and smaller

until he was just the right size a young and handsome soda-cracker man should be!

A new king and queen now live in the soda-cracker castle. They rule the kingdom wisely and well, so that all the people love them. It is a good thing that the handsome young page and the beautiful cracker princess were married and that they are now in charge of the kingdom. The old king is much too busy to be bothered with affairs of government. Each day he sits in the garden, listening to the song of the golden-silver bird. In the evening, when the beautiful bird is sleeping, the old king sometimes tells his soda-cracker grandchildren the story of the handsome young page who became one of the rulers of the soda-cracker kingdom.

The
PRINCESS
and the
TIGER

By Sara Thompson

The king was in a very bad humor, for today his allergies were worse than usual. He sneezed into his big handkerchief and sat down at the long table. At the other end sat his small daughter.

"Well, Princess Suzanne," he said in a hoarse voice, "what have you been doing today?"

"Nothing, Papa," Suzanne said crossly. To tell the truth, Suzanne was bored. She wished something exciting would happen.

Just then the maid set a plate of food in front of the little princess.

Suzanne pushed the plate away. She knew how to cause some excitement.

"I can't eat this awful food!" she said to the maid.

The maid clasped her hands in dismay. Then she rushed over to the headwaiter. "The princess says this food isn't fit to eat!" she cried.

The headwaiter was so disturbed that his spectacles fell off. He rushed into the royal kitchen.

"The princess says there is something wrong with the food!" he said to the cook.

The cook dropped a spoonful of hot gravy. "What!" he screamed. He dashed into the dining room and ran over to the king. "Your Majesty!" he cried. "It isn't true!"

The king scowled. "What do you mean—AH-CHOO—running in here like this? Get back to the kitchen."

As the cook bowed his way back into the kitchen, Suzanne giggled and began to eat her dinner, which she really enjoyed.

An hour later, the king went into the throne room. He was surprised to see that upon every table in the room there sat a vase of beautiful roses.

The king was in a rage. "Who did this?" he shouted. "AH-CHOO! Everyone knows roses make me sneeze."

The king rang his bell. Servants came running.

Pointing to the roses, the king asked, between sneezes, "Whoever brought those in here?"

One man stepped forward and walked bravely up to the king. "I did, Your Majesty," he said. "I am the new gardener, and I did not know you had allergies."

"You should have known!" the king bellowed. "I must punish you."

"Your Majesty," the gardener said, "if you will forgive me, I will give you this ring. It's a magic ring," he said, handing it to the king. "Anyone who wears it can make five wishes come true."

"I don't believe it," said the king. "If this is a magic ring—AH-CHOO—why aren't you rich?"

"You have to be able to wear the ring, Your Majesty. It is too small for any grown person."

"Yes, it is very tiny," said the king. "I don't believe that it is magic, but it is pretty. I forgive you."

Just then Suzanne came into the throne room.

"Suzanne, here is a ring for you," said her father. "Now go play."

"I haven't anyone to play with." Suzanne pouted as she slipped the ring onto her finger.

"Then go to the park and watch the swans."

Suzanne obeyed, but she soon tired of watching the swans. "I wish something exciting would happen," she said aloud.

Just then she heard a terrible roar. A huge tiger was running toward her.

Suzanne scrambled to her feet and ran for a nearby tree.

But try as she would, Suzanne could not climb the tree because her slippers were too slick and her long skirts were in the way.

The tiger was almost upon her. "Oh!" Suzanne sobbed. "I wish I had on the right kind of clothes."

To her amazement, she found that she had on sneakers and jeans.

"How funny!" Suzanne exclaimed as she easily climbed the tree.

She looked down at the tiger. "Where did you come from?" she asked, not expecting an answer.

"From no place," said the tiger. "I wouldn't have hurt you. I was just supposed to give you a taste of excitement."

She must be dreaming! Whoever heard of a talking tiger?

"Well," she said at last. "I wish you would go away now."

"All right," the tiger said agreeably, "but you are being foolish. You have already used up three of your wishes."

More puzzled than ever, Suzanne asked, "What are you talking about?" But the tiger ambled off.

Still trembling, Suzanne climbed down from the tree and walked away. She soon came to the edge of a forest.

There Suzanne noticed a little house she had never seen before. She wondered if any children lived there.

"I wish I had someone to play with," she sighed.

Just then she heard a shout. Out of the house raced four children calling, "Come play with us!"

Suzanne was delighted. She loved playing with her new friends.

At last a woman stuck her head out of the door of the cottage. "Come to supper," she called.

The mother did not seem surprised to see an extra child at the table. She put a plate of boiled potatoes and cold meat in front of Suzanne.

Suzanne pushed the plate away. "I can't eat this!" she said rudely.

"Then don't eat it," the woman said calmly.

Suzanne was hungry. She began to cry.

"Can't you behave yourself?" the woman asked.

"I wish I could," Suzanne said. She was worried that she might lose her new friends.

Now Suzanne did not know that she had made the fifth and last wish on her magic ring. But no sooner had she spoken than she thought of something. A strange feeling came over her, too.

"I must hurry home," she said. "Thank you very much, but my papa will be worried."

From that day on, everyone noticed a change in the princess. She really behaved herself (most of the time), and she made many friends.

The king often teased her about the day she thought a tiger had chased her. But no one understood why she had come home in jeans.

When the gardener heard the story, he just smiled. "Well, sometimes we make some very strange wishes," he said.

300 Oranges

By Alfred Taylor

One morning in the kingdom of Tervia, Kascend the dragon flew toward home with a basket of three hundred oranges. The air was thick with fog. As Kascend flew over Castle Kent, his basket struck the top of a tower and his oranges spilled onto the ground.

When the fog burned away, Kascend flew back to the castle. His oranges were not to be found.

King Alfredo, ruler of Tervia, put on his armor and cautiously approached the dragon. "I am sorry, mighty dragon," the king said. "We ate your oranges for breakfast."

"WHAT!" Kascend bellowed.

"Your oranges—we ate them," the king replied.

"I will stay here until you replace them," Kascend growled. "All three hundred."

"You can't stay here!" the king shouted.

"I can stay here, and I will stay here." Kascend roared so fiercely that King Alfredo was blown out of the courtyard and back into his castle.

One hundred of the king's bravest fighters donned their armor and marched out to battle the mighty dragon. Hours passed, but not one of the brave fighters returned. Worried, the king proclaimed that one hundred gold pieces would be awarded to any man who slew the dragon.

The next morning, news of the king's offer reached Yalt, Tervia's greatest fighter. Yalt arrived at the castle and strode into the courtyard. The king and his subjects were surprised when Yalt left, heading south.

"That fighter," grumbled the king, "is a coward."

Yalt walked south all day, stopping after sunset to build a fire. He put carrots, turnips, and potatoes into a pot. Just as his stew was ready, Yalt saw a creature, half-man and half-horse, hiding behind a bush.

"Hello," said Yalt. "Centaurs are always welcome at my fire."

The centaur walked to the fire and warmed its hands. "Thank you for sharing the fire," it said.

"I am Yalt. If you are hungry, you may also share my stew."

"Where are you heading?" the centaur asked, filling a bowl with stew.

"I am going to Southwood, to gather three hundred oranges for a dragon," Yalt said.

"I'm going that direction, too," the centaur said.

The next morning Yalt rode atop the centaur for many miles. They came upon a wide river and tried to cross, but the current was too swift. So they traveled upstream, looking for a bridge.

After trotting most of the afternoon, they found a red wooden bridge. But as they crossed, a horrible troll with beady eyes jumped out.

"You shall pay me in silver before crossing my bridge," shrieked the giant troll.

"Indeed I shall," said Yalt. He opened his pack and gave two coins to the troll. The fighter and the centaur crossed safely and trotted downstream. At last they arrived at the centaur's home.

Yalt thanked the creature and walked south down a dirt road. At the end of the road, he found an ancient house. The door was unlocked.

Yalt peered into the house. Dust covered the floor. It seemed that the house had been empty for many years. This would do for a night's shelter, he decided, and he stepped inside.

Yalt heard ghostly wailings. Candlesticks floated across the room. He heard a faint voice whisper, "Leave this place. Leave now."

"You wouldn't turn a man out on a cold night, would you?" Yalt asked.

The vaporous form of a young woman appeared. "Aren't you afraid of me?" asked the ghost.

"Why should I fear you? You are a harmless mist," Yalt replied.

"I am not!" the ghost roared. "I'll have you know I've struck fear into the hearts of men for almost a hundred years."

"You don't scare me," Yalt said. The vaporous form crossed the room and began to cry.

"There is no need to cry, my lady," Yalt said softly. "I'm a fighter by profession. I see scary things all the time."

The ghost stopped crying. "If you weren't a fighter, would you be afraid of me?"

"Terrified," Yalt replied.

"If I had played my harp and sung a ghostly song for you, would you have been scared?"

"Horrified," said Yalt. "Why didn't you do that?"

"Many years ago a storm broke the downstairs window. Rain leaked in and ruined all my harp strings."

Yalt walked into the next room and examined the instrument.

"Could you fix it for me?" asked the ghost.

"I'm sure I could," Yalt said. "But I have to leave in the morning. I must find three hundred oranges for Kascend the dragon."

"And just how do you expect to carry all those oranges?" the vaporous form demanded.

"I hadn't actually given it a thought," Yalt said.

"I just happen to own a cart," the ghost said slyly. "You can have it if you fix my harp."

"You have a bargain," Yalt replied with a smile. He repaired the broken window. Then he used his extra bowstrings to replace the strings of the harp.

The ghost played a ballad. It was a song of both joy and sadness, performed with such feeling that Yalt could scarcely keep from crying. When the song ended, the ghost smiled for the first time in a hundred years.

The next morning Yalt took the cart and bid the ghost farewell. He followed another road until he reached the trees of Southwood. Yalt parked the cart beneath a large tree and spent the whole day picking oranges.

Three days later Yalt returned to Castle Kent with his cart of oranges. He found a battle about to commence.

Kascend stood at one end of the courtyard, spewing fire and roaring for his oranges. King Alfredo and one hundred fighters were poised at the other end, ready to charge.

Before the king could give the order to attack, Yalt pushed his cart into the middle of the courtyard. "Stop!" he shouted. "There is no reason to fight. I have three hundred oranges."

The dragon was pleased to see the cart filled with plump fruit. "Thank you, Yalt," said Kascend. "I will take the oranges and return to my lair."

"Wait," said Yalt. "I would speak to you and to the king."

Alfredo proudly rode his horse forward. "If you want me to thank you for gathering those 300 oranges," the king said, "you can forget it because I won't."

"I did not bring them to earn praise, Your Highness. I brought them to settle a dispute between two foolish creatures. Dragons and kings are known for their power and wisdom. Yet both of you forgot the most important lesson about the use of power."

"And what might that be?" the dragon snapped.

"Never use it if you don't have to," Yalt replied.

"The two of you could have settled this dispute in many ways, without taking up arms. You, Your Highness, might have offered payment for the oranges, sent men to gather more."

Yalt turned to the dragon. "And you, Kascend, might have tried to reason with the king. Instead, you acted out of anger."

King Alfredo and Kascend thought for a long while. They looked at each other, and at Yalt. Finally, Alfredo spoke. "Forgive me, both of you," the king said. "I've been fighting for so long I'd forgotten there are better ways to settle differences."

"And I," the dragon said, "should not have allowed anger to color my judgment. I, too, apologize." With that, the great creature lifted the cart of oranges and flew off.

That evening King Alfredo held a feast in Yalt's honor. The king ordered that a statue of Yalt be placed in the Hall of Lords.

The statue was made by the finest sculptor in Tervia, and the inscription at the bottom read: "Here is Yalt, who taught us that the truly courageous fighter is the one who does not fight."

Prince Fennepin's Crown

By June Swanson

"No, no!" cried little Prince Fennepin. "This crown is much too big! It falls over my eyes and I can't see anything. Please find another one!"

"There are no more, sir," said one courtier.

"You've tried all the crowns in the royal vault," said another. "They are all too large."

"But I must have a crown," said Prince Fennepin with a quiver in his voice. "The coronation is next week. How can I become king without a crown? Oh, why do I have to be so much smaller than my father, my grandfather, my great-grandfather, or even my great-great-grandfather? Why couldn't just one of them have had a small head, too?"

The courtiers shook their heads.

Prince Fennepin thoughtfully scratched his small head. "I know!" he shouted with joy. "Call the royal jewelers. They can make a new crown!"

But upon hearing the problem, the royal jewelers looked even sadder than the courtiers.

"I'm sorry, sir," said the master jeweler. "We do not have enough gold or silver to make a crown. It will take thirty days to bring in a new supply and another thirty days to make it. We can have it ready in two months."

"But I *must* have a crown next week," wailed the Prince. "What can I do?"

Again the courtiers and jewelers shook their heads. But no one had an answer.

Word of the problem quickly spread throughout the kingdom. Everyone tried to think of a solution. The next day several people came to see Prince Fennepin.

One of them suggested, "Why not cut one of the bigger crowns down to the right size?"

"That's impossible!" said Prince Fennepin, sadly shaking his small head. "It's against the law to destroy or mar a royal crown."

"Could paper be stuffed inside a crown to make it fit you?" asked another.

"I'll try anything," the prince answered in desperation. The courtiers quickly stuffed a crown with paper. But when Prince Fennepin put it on, he sighed. "This will never do! I look ridiculous!"

People came day and night with more suggestions, but none of them worked. Finally it was the day before the coronation. Dark red velvet banners were ceremoniously draped everywhere. Everything was ready—everything, that is, except the most important thing: the crown!

Poor Prince Fennepin was frantic. "Aren't there any more ideas?" he sobbed.

"No one else has come, sir," said a courtier.

"Only a small girl with a box," said another.

"Well, see what she wants," said the prince.

A courtier came back and whispered, "She says she has a crown for you."

"What? A child with a crown? Come here," said Prince Fennepin gently. "What is your name?"

"Juliana," the girl answered shyly. She came forward slowly. "I have made a crown for you." She lifted the lid of the box and took out a crown, carefully woven of daisies and other wild flowers.

"It is beautiful," the Prince said softly. He put the crown on his small head. "Iit fits perfectly!" He looked in the mirror. "I think I could do it. I could wear this crown for the coronation!"

"But, sir," said a courtier, "it will wilt."

Juliana spoke softly. "I could make a fresh one every day until the royal jewelers have finished the new crown."

"Splendid idea!" cried the Prince. "Our problem is solved! Juliana, I am going to proclaim you my royal crown maker!"

The coronation was beautiful. Everyone agreed that the crown was the perfect thing for Prince Fennepin to wear.

So the new King Fennepin happily wore a fresh flower crown every day until the silver-and-gold one was ready at the end of the summer. The new crown was finished just in time, it turned out, because the flowers were disappeaing for the winter and Juliana, the royal crown-maker was getting ready to start school.

The Princess and the Star

By Toby Speed

Long ago, when the stars first made their designs in the sky and came unstuck from time to time, a princess made a wish.

If I had a star, thought the princess, I'd wear it in my hair, or somewhere.

That evening, while she was outside playing, a shooting star swished overhead. The princess shut her eyes, wished, and POP! Little Star twinkled before her.

"Whee!" said Little Star. "What a ride!"

"Oh, you're perfect!" cried the princess, clapping her hands. But Little Star darted away, lickety-split, and vanished through a castle window.

The princess ran after him, but when she got to the castle, he was gone. Then she heard a giggle from way up high. There was Little Star, twinkling at the top of the turret!

"Tee, hee, hee!" giggled Little Star, dancing on the ledge.

"Silly star," said the princess, laughing. She plucked an apple from a nearby tree and threw it at him, but he cartwheeled out of sight. Grabbing another apple, she scrambled over the windowsill and up the tower stairs.

Around and around, higher and higher she ran, until she came to the room at the top. It was barred and battened and locked up tight. Just a bit of starlight winked and twinkled through a very tiny keyhole in the wooden door.

Without a sound, the princess took a knife from her pocket and cut the apple down through the middle. She put one half of the apple in each hand. Then she sat down, closed her eyes, and pretended to be asleep.

Pretty soon Little Star poked one point through the keyhole and then his whole self. In an instant, the princess leaped up and clapped him inside her apple. Little Star wriggled and danced, but she held on tight.

"Throw me back into the sky," said Little Star.

"No," said the princess.

"If you throw me back," said Little Star, "I will grant your next wish. What do you wish for?"

"Stars," she said. "Little stars. Big stars. Candy stars. Night-light stars. Stars for my buttons. Stars in my pockets. Any kind of stars. I love stars."

"Then plant this apple with me inside," Little Star said. "When you come back tomorrow, you will find a tree full of stars."

"If you can give me such a special tree," said the princess, "I will let you go." And she hurried downstairs to plant the apple.

The next day she came back to find an ordinary-looking apple tree.

"Where are my stars?" wondered the princess. She looked between the branches and under the leaves. No stars anywhere. Then she pulled off an apple and, with her knife, sliced it open from side to side. Right in the middle of each half was a perfect cutout star! The princess opened another apple and another. In each she found two cutout stars.

"Why, you did keep your promise," said the princess, amazed. "Now I'll keep mine. You will be happier in the sky, Little Star."

She dug up Little Star's apple and opened it. At once he streaked upward toward home. All he left behind was his starprint in every apple, and he made sure he was never caught again.

King Frederick the Undignified

By Diana Logue

"I failed again," moaned King Frederick as Lady Lavinia stormed away.

"Yes," agreed the Duke of Hammershaw. "Didn't you know that regal young women don't like to fly kites?"

The king brushed at his dusty trousers. Grass stains smeared both knees, and one knee was torn.

His kite had been flying higher than all the others until he tripped and fell in an unkingly sprawl. Lady Lavinia had left in a huff.

A friend had introduced them, and they had gotten along well as they took a walk through a field near the castle. But when they saw some children flying kites, King Frederick had been unable to resist. His eyebrow began twitching, a sure sign that he was excited.

He borrowed a kite, and politely offered Lady Lavinia the first chance to fly it. Tightening her lips, she declined. While the king dashed across the grass with the red-and-yellow kite soaring behind him, she stood aside, her face frozen grimly.

"And she was such a lovely lady," sighed the duke. "You *must* show a little more dignity."

"Dignity, schmignity," retorted the king, adjusting his crown. "Being a king is hard enough work, without having to be serious, too."

"But roller-skating on the cement border around the south garden?" cried the duke. "When you did that last week, Miss Oglethorpe didn't even wait to say good-bye."

"But it was such fun." The king sighed.

"If you offend all the young women in the kingdom," said the duke, "whom will you marry?"

"Doesn't *anyone* like the things I enjoy?" said the king.

The duke shook his head. "No one over the age of ten it seems."

"What shall I do?" asked the king humbly.

"Be more proper," said the duke, "and . . . more regal."

"How boring," murmured the king. "But I'll try."

For a whole week he tried. He stopped skipping through the castle halls, and he tried not to think about tree houses, fishing poles, or hopscotch. Not even once did he stand on his head. His eyebrow didn't twitch much, but when it did, he tried his utmost to ignore it. By the end of the week, he wasn't even smiling.

"It's a sorry business, being dignified and proper," he said, staring dejectedly at his peanut butter and banana sandwich.

"It's for the best," the duke assured him. "Tomorrow Lady Priscilla is coming to meet you."

The next day, while waiting for Lady Priscilla, the king got out his finger paints (hoping the duke wouldn't find out). He knew the squishy feel of the paints would help him relax.

Twenty minutes later, the duke burst into the room. "She's here!"

"Here?" repeated the king, blinking. "Who?"

"Lady Priscilla," said the duke.

"Maybe she would like to paint, too," said the king hopefully.

"No," said the duke. "And just *look* at yourself!"

The king looked in the mirror and saw a streak of blue paint across one cheek and a glob of orange in his hair. His yellow T-shirt (with KING printed across the front in royal purple letters) was splotched with a rainbow of colors.

He sighed. "I'll go make myself presentable."

Thirty minutes later King Frederick entered the drawing room, wearing his most elegant royal robes. His crown sat on his head, perfectly straight, and he had forced his face into a solemn expression.

The duke introduced the king to a dark-haired young woman who was dressed in a flowing pink gown. "Your Majesty, this is Lady Priscilla."

"I'm very pleased to meet you," the king said formally. "Would you like to join me for a walk through the garden?"

Frederick pretended not to notice that the duke winced at the mention of the garden, where he had already suffered one disgrace.

Priscilla seemed uneasy, and walked stiffly beside him as he showed her the roses, gladiolas, and snap-dragons. He avoided looking at the cement border, which seemed to be begging to be used for a roller-skating race. Being proper made him nervous, and he could sense that Priscilla was miserable, too.

Some children were jumping rope in a corner of the garden. The king's eyebrow began twitching frantically, and he gritted his teeth. Priscilla seemed even more edgy. Neither of them smiled.

Finally, the children's chanting became impossible to ignore; the king's eyebrow was practically dancing a jig. "I must tell you something," he said to Priscilla. "I don't enjoy making polite conversation. What I really would like to be doing is . . . ," he paused and whispered, "jumping rope."

"So would I!" said Priscilla, finally smiling.

In a twinkling, the king took one end of the rope. Priscilla grabbed her long skirts and started jumping to Red Hot Peppers, while the delighted children counted her jumps.

Later, they met the duke on the path back to the castle. "We're going to sail paper airplanes from the top of the tower!" the king announced jubilantly. He was clutching his crown with one hand and Priscilla's hand with the other.

They skipped down the path, waving to the duke, with the king's eyebrow twitching merrily.

From Up Above

By Maia Rodman

To the people who lived on top of the Mountain, the mountain they lived on top of was the very highest in the world.

Each morning and practically every evening and most nights, the people could see nothing at all—or very little of anything. The clouds would hide not only the world below but their own country. Everyone would bump into everyone else. And all you could hear on the streets would be people saying to each other, "Oh, excuse me!"

or "I'm awfully sorry!" Sometimes, but only rarely, since the people of the Mountain were quite polite, you'd hear a gruff voice saying, "Watch where you're going!"

But when the clouds were not there, the people would look down from their Mountain into the valley below. No one ever went there, but everyone knew who lived in the valley.

"Ants live in the valley," the children in school would repeat after their teachers.

"The whole world," the adults would say, "is inhabited by ants. The only place where people live is right here on top of our Mountain."

"We're the only people in the world," the wise men would say.

For centuries and centuries the people of the Mountain believed that only ants lived in the valley below. Not one of them questioned this. That is, not one did until Nina.

Nina happened to be exactly seven years old (since it was her birthday) when she said to her mother, "Mother, I don't believe that ants live in the valley."

Her mother looked very surprised and said, "Hush, Nina, you mustn't say that."

But Nina said to her father, "Father, I don't believe ants live in the valley."

And her father looked at her angrily and said, "Nina, if this were not your birthday, you'd be punished for saying that."

It was the custom of the people of the Mountain to see the king on their birthdays. Nina went alone to the Mountain palace, which stood on the highest point of the Mountain. The king could see better and farther into the valley than anyone else.

When Nina came before the King, instead of saying the usual greeting, "O King, this is my birthday," she said, "O King, I don't believe ants live in the valley."

The king almost toppled from his jeweled throne, he was so surprised by this. He was a round little man, and he could barely reach the floor with his gold slippers. But when Nina said that, the king jumped right down from the throne.

"What have you said?" he demanded.

"I don't believe ants live in the valley," Nina said.

The King shook his round head, and then he shook his round finger at Nina. But before he could say anything, his whole round person was beginning to shake until it shook like a bowl of jelly. The king was laughing.

"Are you laughing at me, O King?" Nina said.

The king just stood there and shook. Pretty soon the whole palace seemed to shake. All of his attendants, not to speak of the queen, the princes, and the princesses, were laughing, too. Everyone in the place always did what the king did.

"I don't think it's funny," Nina said. "I think people like us live in the valley, and not ants. Not ants, at all."

At that the king stopped laughing. The people in the palace stopped, too.

But Nina was not frightened by this great, sudden silence. "I really think people like us live in the valley," she said again.

"What makes you say that?" the king finally asked. His round face was quite red, and his voice shook.

"Because on a clear day I can see all sorts of things," Nina said. "Things like houses and churches and carriages drawn by horses and market women with baskets and even," she laughed, "a school."

The king rushed to the palace window. "Of course. I too see all of that," he said. "But ants live there. Look at their size!"

"But why," Nina asked the king, "would ants build houses and schools and churches? Why would they dress like us?"

"They are still ants!" the king shouted.

"Why?" Nina asked.

"Because everyone says so!" the king screamed.

"But it is not true," Nina said. "Right here on the Mountain there are ants. They are small, and they don't build anything but anthills."

"There is your answer!" the king cried.

"Where?" Nina asked.

"They are small, you said," the king replied. "And the ants down below in the valley are also small."

"But that's how they look to us," Nina said patiently. "They are people, and we see them from way up above. They only seem small to us. We must seem as small to them. Do you think they believe we are ants?"

The king didn't know what he should do. He didn't know whether he should laugh or cry or scream. Since he didn't know what to do, he thought and thought and finally thought the girl was right.

The next day the king and Nina went down from the Mountain into the valley. And what do you think was the first thing they heard?

"The mountain ants are coming!" the valley people were shouting.

But not for long. For when the king and Nina got quite close, the valley people could see that they were people, not ants.

And from that day on, the Mountain people went down to the valley, and the valley people went up to the Mountain. And the ants lived their own lives.

A SONG FOR THE KING

By Marilyn Kratz

King Martin should have been a very happy man. He had a beautiful kingdom and many servants. He had prime ministers to take care of all the affairs of the kingdom, so he never had to work. He had enough gold to buy anything he might want.

But he was not happy. And to make matters worse, he had no idea why he was so unhappy.

Then one day when King Martin was riding through the countryside, he heard a happy sound.

79

It was the happiest sound he had ever heard.

"Stop the coach!" he called to his coachman.

"Who is singing?" he whispered to his page.

"Someone behind those bushes," said the page.

They tiptoed to the bushes and peeked over them. Hoeing a field of corn beyond the bushes was a country lad. His patched shirt and trousers flapped as he worked, and a ragged straw hat bounced atop his head in rhythm with the song he sang.

The king watched and listened until the boy finished hoeing. Then, whistling a merry new tune, the boy walked away.

"I have never seen anyone so happy in all my life," said King Martin.

All the way back to the palace he thought about the boy in the field.

All that night the boy's happy song drifted through his dreams.

The next morning the king sent for his messengers.

"I have decided I need a song to sing so that I can be happy," he told them. "I hereby decree that I will give half my kingdom to the person who writes a song for me that will make me happy."

The messengers carried the decree throughout the kingdom. Soon everyone was writing songs.

Housewives made up songs while they washed dishes. Farmers tried out new tunes on their cows.

Merchants closed their shops early so they would have more time to write songs.

One after another, the people sang their songs for King Martin. Whenever he heard a song he liked, he learned to sing it. But not one of the songs could make him feel happy.

Finally he cried, "No more songs! I'm becoming sadder instead of happier."

King Martin went to his room and spent many days there alone. At last, when his heavy heart was about to break, he remembered the little country lad who sang so merrily.

"That's the song I need!" he shouted. "Page! Have my coach brought around. We are going for a ride in the country."

When they reached the cornfield, the country lad was nowhere in sight, but they could hear him singing nearby. They followed the cheery sound of his song until they found him weeding a pansy patch beside a small cottage.

When the lad saw the king, he stood hastily and stopped singing.

"Please don't stop singing," said King Martin. "I must learn your song."

"My song?" said the boy, quite surprised. "Why, it's just an old folk song my mother taught me, but I will be honored to teach it to you."

King Martin and the country lad sat under a shady tree, and the boy taught the king his song.

Soon King Martin thought he was beginning to feel a little happier. But after he had learned every word of the song, he began to realize it was only his voice that was singing and not his heart.

"Please, Your Majesty," the boy said at last, "may I go back to work now? I want to have the pansy patch all weeded and neat by the time Mother returns. You see, today is her birthday."

"I'm sorry I have taken so much of your time," said King Martin sadly. "May I help you? I haven't anything else to do."

The king rolled up his red velvet sleeves and set to work beside the boy.

"You may use this spade to loosen the soil around each plant," said the boy, when all the weeds had been pulled. "Then I'll water the plants."

Bold little robins came to look for worms in the freshly turned soil. They chirped many merry thank-yous to the king.

The sun warmed the king's back. Perhaps it soaked through to his sad heart. For, without realizing it, the king began to hum. At first it was only an odd tuneless hum, but by the time they were finished working, the king and the country lad were singing loudly together—in harmony!

Suddenly the king shouted, "Why, I'm singing! I'm so happy that I'm singing!"

"It was the work that made you happy," said the boy. "Mother says that the way to be happy is to have important work to do and to do it well."

"Of course!" exclaimed the king. "Why didn't I think of that myself? I've been so unhappy because I've done nothing to make me—or anyone else— happy. But I'm going to change. I promise!"

From that day on King Martin was so busy doing things for others, as well as caring for his own responsibilities, that there was always a song on his lips. But he always found time to visit the country lad each week—to help him weed pansies or hoe corn and to teach *him* a few new songs to sing.

The Island That Had No Birds

By Sister Mary Terese Donze, A.S.C.

Once, many years ago, there was great excitement on the island of Illanoa, home of the birds. The eagle, king of the birds, had announced a meeting, and all the birds were to be there. From every part of the island they flew—blue birds, brown birds, yellow birds, black birds, big birds and little birds—all came to hear the king.

The king stood on a large stone out in an open field. All the birds stood in a big circle around him.

"What does the king want?" asked the little bird with no name, shaking the dust from his feathers.

"Sh-h-h!" scolded an elderly jay. "He will tell us."

The king began to speak. "My little brothers and sisters," he said, looking around at them all, "I have some strange news to tell you."

The birds grew very quiet and listened.

"Many, many days from here, far out in the sea," said the king, "is a beautiful island where there is not one single bird."

The birds looked at one another and lifted their wings in surprise. "No birds? Impossible!"

"It is true," said the king. "No birds. The people there have lovely flowers in their green valleys, and cool, shady forests that smell spicy and fresh. But the people have never seen a bird. They have never heard a bird sing."

All the birds sighed. How sad.

"What a pity," said a robin, shaking her head.

The king looked around at the circle of faces. "Would you like to help these people?" he asked.

"Yes! Yes!" they all answered. And then one after another called out, "Send me!" "Send me, please!" "Send me, your Majesty."

The king called for silence.

"Only one can go," he said.

"Only one! Why only one?"

"The cage the queen of the island sent me is large enough for only one," said the king.

The birds began to fight over who should be picked to go.

Once more the king called for silence.

"We shall have a contest," he said, "and the winner shall go. Each of you practice your song. On contest day the one who sings the best shall go."

All the birds agreed. Each hoped to be the one that would be chosen.

Next day, and every day after, from sunrise to sunset the birds practiced. The island rang with song.

But the little bird with no name did not practice. All day long he sat in a tree and listened to the songs around him. How beautiful they were! He wished all the birds could go to the island.

"Why does the little bird not practice?" asked the other birds one day.

"He is selfish," squawked a parrot. "He does not want to help the people."

"He can't carry a tune," chirped a sparrow.

A starling said, "He's lazy."

The little bird with no name said nothing. He was thinking.

All that day, and the next day, and the day after that, he sat in his nest and listened carefully to all the songs. Then one night he went deep into the woods, and when all the birds were asleep, he practiced. Night after night he did the same thing.

The great day of the contest came. The little bird was tired. He was afraid, too, because he was the youngest of all the birds.

The king stood on the large stone. Once more all the birds sat in a big circle. One by one they came before the king. And how they sang! The air was filled with their music.

At last it was time for the little bird with no name to sing. He stood before the king, shaking with fear. Then he thought of those people far away. Suddenly he wasn't afraid any longer. He started his song.

The king and all the birds listened to the pure beauty that came from the throat of the little bird. After a while the birds began to move uneasily. They looked at one another. They were puzzled. Then they became very angry.

"He's singing my song!" one of them shouted. "And mine!" said another.

"Cheat!" screamed a thrush. "A cheat!" they all echoed. "He mocked us."

"He stole all our songs," said a meadowlark.

"Quiet!" called the king.

The king looked at the little bird.

"You hear what they say about you," he said. "It is true. You sang their songs. You sang them well, but they were not yours. Why did you do this?"

"All my brothers and sisters sing very beautifully," the little bird replied. "I wish they could all go to the people and sing for them. But only one can, so I learned each bird's song for the people who have no birds."

All the birds were very quiet. They thought about what they had heard.

"He is right," called out an old crow.

"Right! Right!" said all the birds. "He can do what we cannot do. He can sing all our songs to the people." They looked at the king. He had stepped from the large stone and was standing before the little bird with no name.

"You shall carry our songs to the people in the lovely, green valleys," the king said. "But you shall no longer be nameless. From this day on you shall be known as the *mockingbird* because you copied the songs of all the birds. But do not be afraid. Harsh as it sounds, your new name will be a badge of honor, for you earned it by doing a loving deed."

And so it is. Today everyone knows and loves the sweet-throated mockingbird.

A Shovel, an Ax, and a Ladder

By Walter K. Putney

Many years ago, in the famous Black Forest region of Europe, a princess named Eloise was stolen from her father's palace and carried deep into the woods. Because nobody had ever found a way out of the Black Forest, her captors did not guard her every minute. So she wandered around by herself, watching the birds, picking flowers, and feeding the squirrels, for she loved nature. So friendly did all wild creatures become that it was not uncommon to see Princess Eloise walking down the path with a squirrel on her shoulder or a bird perched on her finger.

One day, as she sat on an old log, watching some baby wood mice playing close by, she was surprised to hear a voice.

"Are you really a princess who was stolen and carried away by the raiders?"

Eloise turned and saw a funny little fellow seated on the log. He wore a cocked hat and had long ears that looked like the rabbits Eloise played with. His arms and legs were very long and thin. His smile was very friendly.

Eloise replied, "Yes, I was a princess once." Then she sighed before continuing, "But I do not suppose that I shall ever see my father or mother again. Who are you? And why are you asking me such a question?"

"I am one of the good elves that live here in the Black Forest. We always try to help those who are kind to the wood folk. Would you like us to help you escape from here?"

"Oh, if you only would!" Eloise exclaimed. "How could you do it? I have been told that no prisoner has ever escaped from this place."

"Be of good cheer. Keep on feeding your friends, the birds and squirrels and other small animals. Maybe someday you will see me again."

For several days Eloise went out into the woods, carrying food to her forest friends and looking about to see if she could catch a glimpse of that good elf again. Then, one morning, as she sat on her favorite log, she heard a whisper.

"Eloise, how would you like to escape today?"

"Today!" she exclaimed. "Oh, if I only could. Have my captors gone away so that they will not learn of my escape?"

"You must start at once," said the good elf. "Your captors are still near. But if you travel toward the sun, I am sure you will get away."

"But I see no path in the direction of the sun. How can I make my way through that dense woodland?"

"Here are three tools with which a path can be made—a shovel, an ax, and a ladder. See them right at my feet?" said the good elf. "You have not seen these tools before because, until you use each one, it cannot be seen by any person. No matter how much anybody may plead with you to use these tools, never let them out of your possession."

The good elf gave Eloise the shovel, ax, and ladder. As she got ready to start on her journey in the direction of the sun, the good elf spoke once more.

"Sometime you may come upon an obstacle that seems too big for you to overcome. If such a difficulty occurs, you may call upon the good elves to help you. But do not forget—you can get help from the elves only three times. Now, Eloise, good-bye and good luck to you."

So Eloise began walking toward the sun, and to her surprise, the underbrush turned aside so that she could walk through it. After a few hours she came to a wide river that rushed rapidly along.

"What shall I do now?" Eloise asked herself. "My shovel and ax and ladder cannot help me cross this stream."

Then she heard a pounding sound. Turning, she saw Old Beaver slapping his big, flat tail on the ground. In a few moments dozens of beavers came in response to this sound. In less time than it takes to tell, the beavers were cutting down small trees and carrying them to the river. Soon a dam was made, and Eloise was able to walk across and reach the other side. She turned to thank his beaver friends, but they had disappeared into the underbrush.

Eloise walked on and on until the sun, with a bright purple farewell, sank beneath the horizon. She wondered if she should keep on traveling. Then she heard the hooting of an owl. Looking up, she saw the very same owl that she had fed and made friends with when she had been a captive. "How strange a sound that owl is making,"

Eloise wondered aloud. "What could he want?" Then she thought, "Maybe he wishes me to follow him. I'll do so at once."

That was just what the owl wanted. He led Eloise to an overhanging rock and a nice, cozy bed of grasses and leaves. She was very tired and slept until noon the next day. Then she picked up the shovel, ax, and ladder and continued her journey. In a few hours she came to a great wall that was so high and long she became terribly discouraged.

"Oh dear," she thought, "my ladder will not reach the top of that wall. If I tried to climb from the end of the ladder to the top, I know I would fall and be killed. What can I do now? I must ask for help from the good elves."

So she asked for help. In no time the same funny little elf sat down beside her.

"Well, well, what is the matter?" asked the good elf. "Did you try to use your ax and cut a hole in the wall? Try it now, before it becomes too hard."

Eloise tried, but she could cut only a short way into the wall. In despair she turned to the good elf. "What shall I do now?"

"My goodness!" exclaimed the good elf, and then he laughed. "What do you suppose that shovel is for? Surely we did not give it to you just so that you could look at it!"

Eloise thought for a moment. Then a bright gleam came into her eyes. She took the shovel and started to dig under the wall. It was hard work, but Eloise kept at it. In a few minutes the shovel broke through the wall, and she saw that she was on the grounds of the royal palace. With lightened step she hastened to the palace to let her mother and brothers and sisters know that she was alive and well. The good elf ran beside her and spoke a few last words to Eloise.

"Your father, the king, has died, and you are now queen. Remember—you will succeed in being a good, just ruler only while you have with you a shovel, an ax, and a ladder to overcome all difficulties. For there are none so great that they cannot be overcome. If you find something too tall to climb over, try cutting through it. If that fails, you can, as you have learned, dig under it. Good-bye!"